The Blue Pearls

For Elise's children Peter, Claire, and Shannon — E. S. W.
To my family and friends — V. G.

Barefoot Books
37 West 17th Street
4th Floor East
New York, New York 10011

This book is printed on 100% acid-free paper
Typeset in Garamond Book 15pt on 26pt leading
Illustrations prepared in acrylics and mixed media

Graphic design by designsection, England
Color separation by Color Gallery, Malaysia
Printed in Hong Kong/China by South China Printing Co. (1988) Ltd.

1 3 5 7 9 8 6 4 2

U.S. Cataloging-in-Publication Data (Library of Congress Standards)

Warfel, Elizabeth Stuart.
The blue pearls / written by Elizabeth Stuart Warfel ;
illustrated by Véronique Giarrusso
[32]p. : col. ill. ;   cm.
Summary: Inspired by a dream the author has shortly before her daughter
dies, this is the story of the passage through death from the perspective
of a small angel.
ISBN 1-902283-78-3
1. Bereavement – Fiction. 2. Grief in children. I. Giarrusso, Véronique, ill.
II. Title.
[E] –dc21   2000   AC   CIP

ACKNOWLEDGMENTS
With special thanks to Elise's sister Lesley,
and Elise's friends, especially Msgr. Connolly,
Kathleen, Janet D., Janet H., and Consuelo.

The Blue Pearls

written by **Elizabeth Stuart Warfel**

illustrated by **Véronique Giarrusso**

walk
the way of wonder...
Barefoot Books

he angels were assembled in a circle, occupying themselves with something very special. Spread out in front of the group were lengths and lengths of

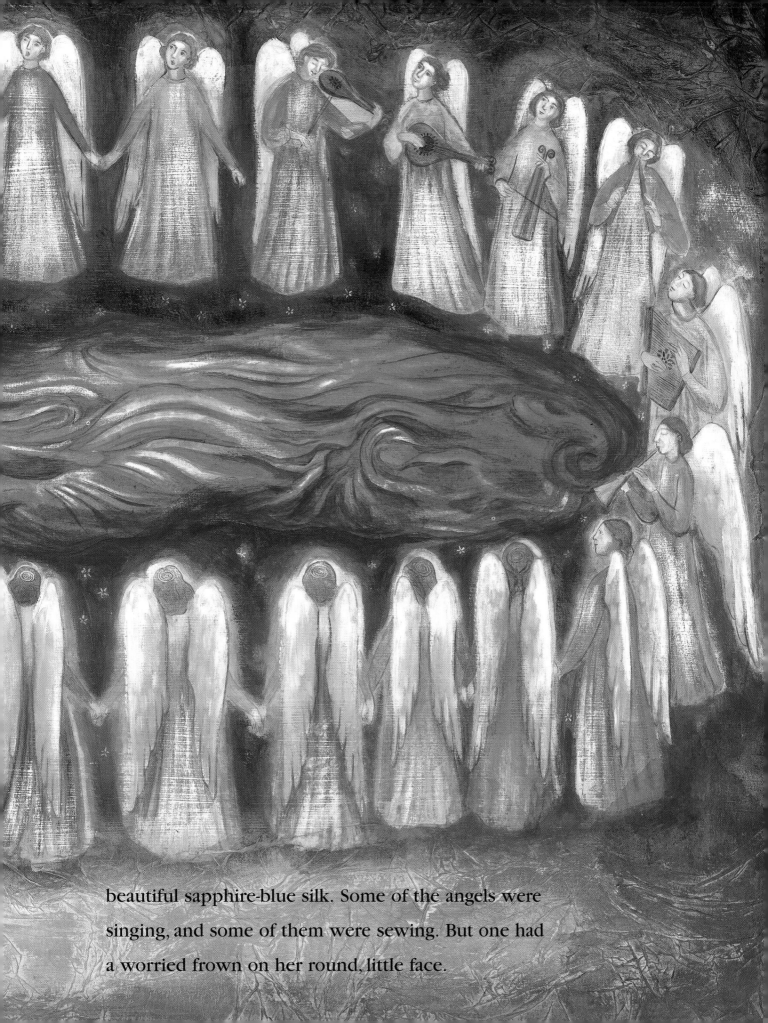

beautiful sapphire-blue silk. Some of the angels were
singing, and some of them were sewing. But one had
a worried frown on her round, little face.

"When is she coming?" asked the round-faced angel. "When does Elise come?"

"Quiet, Angelica. She is still teaching, and it's not yet time."

"But we've already started the blue dress, and I can't see her anywhere, not anywhere."

"She's not ready, and neither is the dress," said the head angel. "There is a lot of work still to do, and we must have blue pearls to put around her earthly heart and her heavenly soul."

The whole group of sewing angels looked up from their work, and cried with one voice, "But there aren't any blue pearls. Pearls don't come in blue. They are white and sometimes they are pink or gray, but not blue."

The head angel, who was a little taller and straighter than the others, fluttered her wings, which is what angels do when they are about to begin an important task. The seamstresses waited, all a-twitter, as their leader spoke. "I am going to the great oysters to ask them to make some pearls for Elise's dress."

The head angel's journey took her past all the marvels
of nature. She flew over Uluru and the Grand Canyon;
she flew over mighty seas and lush rainforests; she flew
over the towering white mountains of the Himalayas
and on past the vast, sun-baked deserts of the Middle
East. As she flew, she looked down as well on the
great works of humans; she saw the pyramids in

Egypt and the Parthenon in Greece. She saw the Taj
Mahal in India and the Alhambra in Spain. And she
saw the huge industrial cities of the modern world,
with their busy offices and crowded freeways. The
head angel rejoiced at all the beautiful things she
saw, but she felt sad, too, that humans forget who
they really are — sometimes.

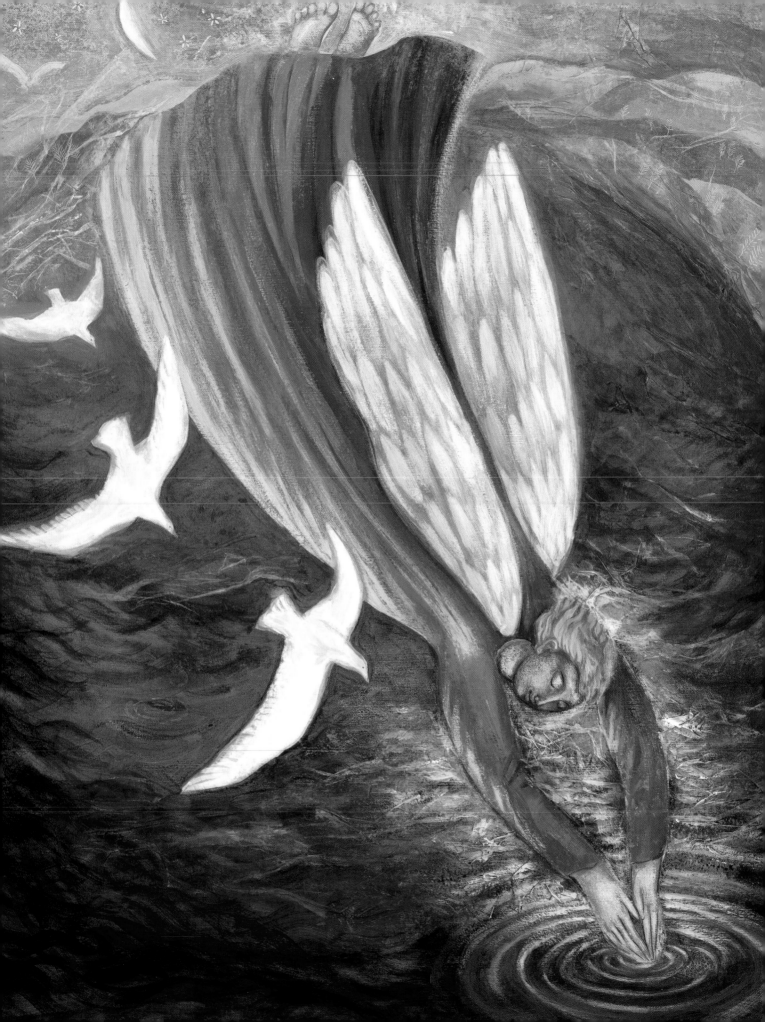

The head angel was starting to lose herself in the strange dreams that came to her when she entered the world of earthly folk. She reminded herself why she was there, and headed on, down, down, down, to the home of the great oysters.

The oysters were surprised at the angel's request, and said it could not be done. They could make white pearls, and they could make pearls that would reflect all the colors of the rainbow, but as for blue pearls — that was quite unheard of. The head angel thought for a bit and realized that she needed help from a higher power.

So she went right to the top with her request.

"Why, certainly it can be done and so it shall," said the higher power. "But first you must return home and try again. Listen to the sounds around you, and you will know in your heart where the pearls are to be found."

The head angel was very wise and she was used to organizing the other angels, but she never stopped learning herself. She thanked the higher power and headed back the way she had come.

Far away, down in the sea, beyond the land of the great oysters, was the home of the very small oysters. Too small to be of any interest to the great ones, they spent most of their days feeling sad. All except one, who was the smallest of them all. On special days, when the tides were right, his sweet, small, encouraging voice could be

heard singing as far away as the land of the great
oysters … and sometimes beyond.

"What is that?" asked one great oyster, as the head
angel flew back down toward the ocean.

"What is that?" echoed the higher power.

The head angel heard the voice, too. "What is that?" she wondered, as she flew over the sea. She followed the voice down, down, down, past the beds of the great oysters. Down, down, down, closer and closer to the colony of very small oysters, who were gathered around their smallest member. As the smallest oyster sang, a halo of soft blue light glowed all around him.

The head angel scooped up the halo of blue light, for angels can do such things, tucked it inside the creature's shell and spoke:

"Smallest oyster, who can sing to make us happy, it is you who shall make the blue pearls for Elise's dress."

Then all the very small oysters rejoiced and began to sing together as one.

"Good-bye," said the head angel.

"Good-bye and thank you," said the very small oysters.

The head angel returned to the other angels, who were waiting for her with great excitement.

"Where are the blue pearls?" asked one angel.

"Patience. They will be ready when Elise has finished her teaching, as I told you before. Just as we shall have to teach her as our child, so she has to teach her own children before she can join us. Patience. It will be soon."

The head angel called for Angelica, with her round face and bright eyes, and asked her to go and collect the blue pearls.

Angelica had never had such a responsible job before. With a fluffing and a fluttering of her wings, she got ready and set off.

As she flew, an idea came to her. She felt a little
naughty, but she changed course.

A moment later, Angelica was at Elise's house
high on the hill.

Angelica flew quietly into Elise's bedroom. She could see right away that Elise was teaching her three children. She listened quietly as Elise told the children that she would only be with them a little longer, and she watched as Elise gathered them into her arms and wept with them. Angelica sent waves of angel courage to Elise and listened again. This time Elise told them that what is most important in life is loving and being loved; being rich or famous or busy does not really matter. And she told her children that she loved them very much.

Angelica blew Elise a special angel kiss and gave her
an extra earth week to play with her children. Then
she darted off to the land of the very small oysters
to fetch the blue pearls.

For the next week, the seamstresses worked every day. First, they cut and sewed the dress. Then they stitched the blue pearls onto the bodice, one for each child, making sure that everything was just right.

At last, the beautiful blue dress was ready. It shimmered and shone in the soft light, and all the angels agreed that it was the most beautiful dress they had ever made.

One morning, the head angel said, "It's time."

All the angels gathered together, fluffing and fluttering their wings.

"She's coming, she's coming!" cried Angelica.

"She's here!"

Author's Note

This story is inspired by the example of my daughter Elise, who died of cancer in 1993. Shortly before her death, I had a dream, and from the dream came the story, which is offered to everyone who reads it, but especially to children who are suffering from terminal illness, and to the children of parents who are terminally ill.

I saw you, my daughter Elise, in a dream. A beautiful girl in a sapphire-blue dress of such a heavenly color that it defies all description. Almost more luminous than the shimmer of the silk was the smile on your face. I heard you laugh and you drew my attention to your feet dancing beneath that wondrous dress. Your feet pivoted round and round and round. The more you turned, the more you laughed. You never became dizzy and you never ceased to laugh and smile.

As I watched you, in my dream, I noticed your soft white shoulders, and above and around your neck, a tiny ruff like a starched white muslin wreath, crimped and full, setting off your vivacious face. You were going to speak, then changed your mind. And billowing up your dress with your fingers, you turned — the fullness of the fabric following your movement as if in a suspended motion — and looked over your shoulder and waved your hand to me.

For the first time I noticed a long passageway full of light and brightness such as I had never seen before. The light embraced you and you were gone.

Elizabeth Stuart Warfel